RACHEL

A MODERN TALE OF LOVE AND SISTERHOOD

WOMEN OF THE BIBLE FICTION
BOOK 3

KAYLA LOWE

Want a free book? Sign up to my newsletter to get my award-winning book for free! www.authorkaylalowe.com

MORE OF MY BOOKS

<u>Series</u>

<u>Charms of the Chaste Court</u>

A Courtship in Covent Garden
Whispers in Westminster
Romance in Regent's Park
Serenade on Strand Street
Treasure in Tower Bridge

<u>Sweet Honey by the Sea</u>

<u>The Beekeeper's Secret (Book 1)</u>
<u>A Royal Honeycomb (Book 2)</u>
<u>Bees in Blossom (Book 3)</u>
<u>Honeyed Kisses (Book 4)</u>
<u>Blooming Forever (Book 5)</u>

<u>Strawberry Beach Series</u>

<u>Beachside Lessons (Book 1)</u>
<u>Beachside Lessons (Book 2)</u>
<u>Beachside Lessons (Book 3)</u>

Panama City Beach Series

Sun-Kissed Secrets (Book 1)
Sun-Kissed Secrets (Book 2)
Sun-Kissed Secrets (Book 3)

The Tainted Love Saga

Of Love and Deception (Book 1)
Of Love and Family (Book 2)
Of Love and Violence (Book 3)
Of Love and Abuse(Book 4)
Of Love and Crime (Book 5)
Of Love and Addiction (Book 6)
Of Love and Redemption (Book 7)

Standalones

Maiden's Blush

Poetry

Phantom Poetry
Lost and Found

CHAPTER 1

Rachel wakes from sleep as the winter dawn light slants through her bedroom window. A vision of beauty and poise, she rises resiliently, as if invigorated by the new day with all its promise and possibilities.

She prepares mentally and physically for the important business event where she will network with the city's elite entrepreneurs. Glancing at her reflection, Rachel sees a polished, elegant woman, tall and graceful, whose outward appearance commands attention. She adorns herself in a designer outfit that exudes power and status. Secretly though, Rachel fears this facade masks the hidden insecurities lurking beneath the surface—the tremendous pressure to maintain her perfect, successful image at all costs.

Across town, Leah begins her day with quiet grace, inner goodness radiating from her like a serene glow. Where Rachel mesmerizes with magnetism and charisma, Leah captivates with calming compassion and keen intuition. Heading to work at the non-profit where she pours her heart into helping the underprivileged, Leah's simple, comfortable attire reflects her humble demeanor and gentle spirit.

As Rachel strides into her high-rise office, Leah slips behind the scenes at the organization she serves, both working in their own spheres. The contrasting sisters, each extraordinary in her own way, set about their divergent days.

Rachel reviews her marketing proposals with a critical eye, aiming for flawless campaigns to impress at the networking event. Her brilliant mind hums, strategizing how to outshine the competition. Yet a fleeting unease gnaws at her. Is this relentless ambition distancing her from what matters most? From family? From herself?

Miles from the glittering towers of commerce, Leah immerses herself in advocacy for vulnerable children, a light illuminating dark corners of injustice. She emanates empathy and understanding, a soothing presence for troubled souls. But in rare moments alone, doubt creeps in, an echo of her parents' disapproval. Why can't she command crowds like Rachel? Be the star, not the shadow?

The White sisters, bound by blood, remain worlds apart as they follow their true paths through life. Rachel ascends to dizzying corporate heights while Leah uplifts the downtrodden with selfless devotion. Each admirable, each incomplete without the other to lend balance and perspective. Their ultimate challenge lies in bridging the distance between them to forge an unbreakable bond transcending all measures of success.

Jacob Bennett stepped out of the sleek black car that had ferried him from the airport, his polished shoes making contact with the bustling city sidewalk. He paused for a moment, inhaling deeply as he surveyed the towering skyscrapers that stretched endlessly toward the heavens. The urban landscape hummed with an electric energy, a palpable current of ambition and opportunity that resonated deep within his entrepreneurial spirit.

As he strode purposefully toward his hotel, Jacob's thoughts wandered to the upcoming networking event that had drawn him to this metropolis. He had built a formidable reputation in the culinary world, his chain of upscale restaurants renowned for their innovative cuisine and impeccable service. Yet, he knew that complacency was the enemy of progress. To truly expand his empire, he needed to forge new connections, to immerse himself in the dynamic tapestry of the city's business elite.

A gentle breeze ruffled Jacob's carefully styled hair as he navigated the crowded streets, his mind already charting the course of his evening. He envisioned himself mingling effortlessly with the crème de la crème of the corporate world, his natural charisma and keen business acumen allowing him to forge valuable alliances. And yet, beneath the veneer of confidence, a flicker of uncertainty danced in his piercing blue eyes. Success had come at a price, demanding sacrifices that left him questioning the true meaning of fulfillment.

As he entered the opulent lobby of his hotel, Jacob's gaze fell upon a striking poster advertising the very event he had come to attend. The image of a woman, her face obscured but her presence commanding, caught his attention. There was something about her, an aura of strength and determination that resonated with his own drive. In that fleeting moment, Jacob felt an inexplicable pull, a sense that this mysterious figure held the key to a profound revelation.

With renewed purpose, Jacob made his way to his suite, his mind consumed by thoughts of the impending gathering. He knew that this event held the potential to shape the trajectory of his future, both professionally and personally. As he meticulously prepared for the evening, selecting an impeccably tailored suit and rehearsing his elevator pitch, Jacob couldn't shake the lingering image of the enigmatic woman from the poster. Little did he know that their paths were destined to intertwine, setting in motion a chain of events that would challenge everything he thought he knew about success, love, and the delicate balance between ambition and authenticity.

CHAPTER 2

Rachel glided through the bustling ballroom, her elegant emerald gown shimmering under the chandelier's soft glow. Her eyes scanned the crowd, a sea of influential faces and potential connections. She knew this was her element, where she could dazzle with her wit and charm her way to new opportunities.

As she gracefully navigated the room, Rachel felt a prickling sensation on the back of her neck. She turned, her gaze locking with a pair of striking blue eyes from across the room. The man, tall and handsome with an air of quiet confidence, held her gaze for a moment before offering a subtle smile. Rachel felt a flutter in her chest, a rare sensation for someone so accustomed to being in control.

She turned back to her conversation partner, her mind momentarily drifting to the mysterious stranger. *Who was he*, she wondered, *and what secrets lay behind those piercing eyes?* Rachel shook off the thought, refocusing on the task at hand—networking her way to the top.

As the evening progressed, Rachel found herself in a lively discussion with a group of industry leaders. She artfully wove anecdotes and insights, captivating her audience with her sharp intellect and magnetic presence. Just as she delivered a particularly witty remark, a familiar voice chimed in from behind her.

"I couldn't help but overhear," the voice said, smooth and warm. "That was a brilliant point about the future of marketing."

Rachel turned, coming face-to-face with the blue-eyed stranger from earlier. Up close, she could appreciate the chiseled lines of his jaw and the warmth of his smile.

"Jacob Bennett," he introduced himself, extending a hand. "I've been admiring your work from afar. Your campaigns are truly innovative."

"Rachel White," she replied, shaking his hand firmly. "And thank you. I take pride in pushing boundaries."

As they delved into conversation, Rachel found herself drawn to Jacob's quiet confidence and thoughtful insights. He spoke passionately about his culinary ventures, his eyes lighting up as he described his journey from humble beginnings to restaurant mogul. Rachel, in turn, shared her own trials and triumphs, surprised at how easily the words flowed between them.

Time seemed to stand still as they exchanged ideas and aspirations, their ambition and drive palpable in the air. Rachel felt a rare connection, a kindred spirit in this man who understood the thrill of the climb and the hunger for success.

As the evening wound down, Rachel and Jacob reluctantly parted ways, but not before exchanging contact information and a promise to continue their riveting conversation. Rachel walked out into the cool night air, her mind abuzz with new possibilities and the lingering electricity of their encounter. She knew, deep down, that this was just the beginning of something extraordinary.

Leah navigated the bustling community center, a tray of homemade cookies balanced precariously in her hands. The room hummed with the chatter of volunteers and the laughter of children, a vibrant tapestry of hope and compassion. As she wove through the crowd, offering treats and gentle smiles, Leah couldn't help but feel a sense of belonging, a connection to something greater than herself.

Lost in thought, she didn't notice the tall figure approaching until they collided, sending cookies tumbling to the floor. Strong hands grasped her shoulders, steadying her as she regained her balance. Leah looked up, an apology on her lips, and found herself gazing into a pair of striking blue eyes.

"I'm so sorry," the man said, his voice smooth and warm. "I should've been watching where I was going."

"No, no, it's my fault," Leah insisted, kneeling to gather the fallen cookies. "I was in my own little world."

He crouched down beside her, helping to salvage what they could. As they worked, their hands brushed briefly, sending a jolt of electricity through Leah's veins. She glanced up, surprised by the sudden flutter in her chest, and caught a glimpse of his kind smile.

"I'm Jacob, by the way," he offered, standing up and brushing the crumbs from his hands.

"Leah," she replied softly, a faint blush coloring her cheeks. "And thank you, for your help."

Jacob's eyes crinkled at the corners as he smiled. "It's my pleasure. I'm just happy to be here, doing my part."

Leah nodded, understanding the sentiment all too well. "It's a wonderful feeling, isn't it? Being part of something bigger than yourself?"

"Absolutely," Jacob agreed, his gaze lingering on hers for a moment. "And speaking of doing my part, I should probably get back to it."

"Of course," Leah said, stepping aside. "I won't keep you."

With a final smile and a nod, Jacob disappeared into the crowd, leaving Leah with a tray of crumbled cookies and a curious warmth in her chest. She shook her head, dismissing the fleeting attraction as nothing more than a momentary spark, and returned to her duties, unaware of the man's growing connection with her sister.

As the event wound down and the volunteers began to disperse, Leah couldn't help but reflect on the brief encounter. Jacob's easy smile and genuine warmth had touched something deep within her, a longing for a connection she hadn't known she craved. But as quickly as the feeling had come, she pushed it aside, reminding herself that her purpose lay in serving others, not in chasing after her own desires.

With a sigh, Leah gathered her belongings and headed for the exit, her heart heavy with the weight of unspoken hopes and unacknowledged dreams. Little did she know that the threads of fate were already weaving a complex web, one that would soon ensnare her heart and test the bonds of sisterhood like never before.

CHAPTER 3

Rachel tucked a stray auburn lock behind her ear as she entered the upscale bistro, her high heels clicking against the polished hardwood floor. Scanning the room, her piercing green eyes landed on Jacob, who rose from his seat with a warm smile. His tailored suit accentuated his athletic build, and Rachel felt a flutter of anticipation as she approached him.

"Rachel, you look stunning as always," Jacob said, his blue eyes sparkling with admiration. He pulled out her chair, his fingers brushing against her shoulder, sending a shiver down her spine.

"Thank you, Jacob. It's always a pleasure to see you," Rachel replied, her tone confident and charming. As they settled into their seats, Rachel couldn't help but notice the envious glances from other diners, their eyes drawn to the striking couple.

The waiter appeared, offering menus and a wine list. Jacob selected a vintage Cabernet Sauvignon, his knowledge of fine wines impressing Rachel. As they perused the menu, their conversation flowed effortlessly, transitioning from business matters to more personal topics. Rachel found herself captivated by Jacob's wit and intellect, his insights both thought-provoking and engaging.

As the lunch progressed, Rachel sensed a shift in the atmosphere. Jacob's gaze lingered on her a moment longer than necessary, his hand brushing against hers as he passed the salt shaker. The chemistry between them was palpable, a current of electricity that seemed to charge the very air they breathed.

"I must admit, Rachel," Jacob said, his voice low and intimate, "I find myself looking forward to these lunches more and more. Your company is truly a delight."

Rachel's heart swelled with satisfaction, a smile playing at the corners of her lips. "I feel the same way, Jacob. It's rare to find someone who can keep up with me both professionally and personally."

As they shared a decadent chocolate dessert, Rachel couldn't help but imagine a future with Jacob by her side. He seemed to embody everything she had ever wanted in a partner—ambition, sophistication, and a deep understanding of her needs.

Across town, Leah sat in her modest apartment, nursing a cup of chamomile tea. Her thoughts drifted to Rachel, no doubt enjoying another lavish lunch with the illustrious Jacob Bennett. Despite the genuine happiness she felt for her sister, Leah couldn't shake the profound loneliness that had taken root in her heart.

It was just her luck the one man who caught her eye was enamored with her sister.

Leah's eyes wandered to the framed photographs on her bookshelf, snapshots of happier times when the two sisters were inseparable. Now, it seemed as though an invisible chasm had opened up between them, with Rachel's success and glamorous lifestyle leaving Leah behind in the shadows.

As the sun began to set, casting a warm glow

through her window, Leah sighed, her fingers tracing the delicate petals of a potted African violet on her windowsill. The solitary bloom seemed to mirror her own existence—beautiful, yet often overlooked in favor of more extravagant displays.

Jacob found himself at yet another charitable event, his mind still lingering on the captivating Rachel White. As he navigated the sea of well-dressed attendees, his gaze settled upon a familiar face—Leah, the quiet yet kind-hearted woman he had briefly encountered at previous gatherings.

Leah stood alone, her delicate features illuminated by the soft glow of the chandeliers. She seemed content in her solitude, observing the crowd with a gentle smile that hinted at a deep well of compassion within her. Jacob felt an inexplicable pull towards her, drawn to the serene aura that surrounded her like a comforting embrace.

As he approached, Leah looked up, her hazel eyes widening in recognition. "Mr. Bennett," she greeted him warmly, her voice soft and melodic. "It's a pleasure to see you again."

Jacob returned her smile, feeling an unexpected sense of ease in her presence. "Please, call me Jacob. I've been hoping to run into you tonight, Leah. Your dedication to these charitable causes is truly admirable."

Leah ducked her head modestly, a faint blush coloring her cheeks. "I believe we all have a responsibility to make a difference, no matter how small," she replied, her words filled with quiet conviction.

As they fell into comfortable conversation, Jacob found himself captivated by Leah's gentle spirit and the depth of her compassion. She spoke of her work with underprivileged children, her eyes sparkling with a passion that seemed to illuminate her from within.

In the midst of their exchange, Jacob's thoughts drifted to Rachel, the woman who had initially captured his attention with her confidence and ambition. Yet, as he stood beside Leah, he couldn't help but feel a different kind of connection—one based on shared values and a mutual desire to make the world a better place.

As the evening drew to a close, Jacob found himself reluctant to part ways with Leah. Her quiet strength and unwavering kindness had touched something deep within him, leaving him with a newfound appreciation for the beauty of a gentle soul.

Unbeknownst to Jacob, the threads of fate had begun to weave a tapestry that would forever intertwine his path with those of the White sisters. As he bid Leah farewell, he couldn't shake the feeling that their brief encounter had set in motion a chain of events that would change the course of their lives in ways none of them could have anticipated.

CHAPTER 4

The chandeliers glistened, casting a warm glow over the ballroom filled with Atlanta's elite. Jacob Bennett, dashing in his tailored tuxedo, stood at the center of the dance floor, his eyes locked on Rachel White as she glided towards him in a shimmering emerald gown. The murmur of the crowd faded as he took her hand, his heart pounding with the weight of the moment.

"Rachel," he began, his voice steady despite the nerves fluttering in his stomach. "From the moment I met you, I knew my life would never be the same. Your grace, your brilliance, your passion for making a difference—it all captivates me. I can't imagine spending another day without you by my side."

Slowly, he sank to one knee, producing a velvet

box from his pocket. Rachel's hand flew to her mouth, her eyes widening as he opened the box to reveal a dazzling diamond ring. "Rachel White, will you marry me?"

The room erupted in applause as Rachel, tears glistening in her eyes, whispered a breathless "Yes." Jacob slipped the ring onto her finger, rising to pull her into a tender embrace. As they swayed to the music, Rachel's mind raced with visions of their future together—a life of influence, of prestige, of shared purpose. This was the moment she had dreamed of, the affirmation that she had truly made it.

Miles away, Leah White sat in her modest apartment, her phone illuminating her face as she scrolled through the flood of photos and well-wishes on Rachel's social media. A bittersweet smile played at the corners of her mouth as she typed out a congratulatory comment, her fingers hesitating over the 'send' button.

She was happy for her sister, truly. But as she stared at the image of Jacob, his eyes alight with love and devotion, a dull ache bloomed in her chest. It wasn't just the reminder of her own singleness, the nagging fear that she would always be overlooked in favor of her more accomplished sibling. No, it was something deeper, a longing she had never quite allowed herself to acknowledge.

Leah had always been drawn to Jacob's warmth, his quiet strength, the way he seemed to truly see and appreciate the person beneath the surface. In another life, perhaps, she might have been the one to capture his heart. But as she watched the video of him slipping the ring onto Rachel's finger, she knew that door had closed forever.

With a sigh, Leah sent the comment and closed her phone, her gaze drifting to the window where the city lights twinkled like distant stars. She whispered a silent prayer, asking for the strength to be content with what she had, to find her own path to love and fulfillment. For now, she would focus on being the supportive sister, the loyal friend, the woman of faith she had always strived to be. The rest, she trusted, would come in God's own time.

Jacob stood at the edge of the ballroom, his gaze sweeping over the sea of elegantly dressed attendees. The charity gala was in full swing, a glittering tableau of wealth and philanthropy, but his mind was far from the festivities. He absently twisted the silver band on his finger, a tangible reminder of his commitment to Rachel.

Across the room, he spotted a familiar figure, her dark hair swept into a simple updo, her sky blue dress a stark contrast to the ostentatious gowns surrounding her. *Leah.* As if sensing his gaze, she glanced up, their eyes meeting briefly before she quickly looked away.

Jacob felt a strange tug in his chest, an inexplicable draw to the quiet, unassuming woman who had always lingered in the background of his life. Excusing himself from his current conversation, he made his way towards her, weaving through the throng of partygoers.

"Leah," he greeted warmly, his hand coming to rest on her elbow. "I didn't expect to see you here."

She looked up at him, her hazel eyes wide with surprise. "Jacob. I...I've been volunteering with this organization for a while now. They do great work with underprivileged children."

He smiled, a genuine warmth suffusing his

features. "That sounds like you. Always thinking of others."

A faint blush colored her cheeks, and she ducked her head. "I just try to do what I can. It's nothing compared to the generous donations from people like you and Rachel."

Jacob frowned slightly, his grip on her elbow tightening. "Don't sell yourself short, Leah. Your time and dedication are just as valuable as any monetary contribution."

She met his gaze then, a flicker of something unreadable in her eyes. "Thank you, Jacob. That means a lot."

As they fell into easy conversation, discussing the charity's latest initiatives and their shared passion for giving back, Jacob felt a growing sense of unease. The way Leah's face lit up when she spoke of her volunteer work, the gentle compassion in her voice, the subtle brush of her hand against his arm...it all felt so natural, so right.

And yet, the weight of the ring on his finger served as a constant reminder of his reality. He was engaged to Rachel, the woman he had chosen to build a life with. So why did being with Leah feel like coming home?

As the evening wore on and they found themselves drawn into each other's orbit time and again, Jacob couldn't shake the feeling that he was standing on the edge of something profound, something that could change everything. And deep down, in a place he barely dared to acknowledge, he wondered if he was ready to take that leap.

CHAPTER 5

Leah hunched over her cluttered desk, pen poised above the legal documents before her. The cramped office seemed to close in around her as she pored over the case file, searching for any detail that might help her client—a single mother fighting for custody of her children. Leah's tired eyes scanned the pages, the words blurring together as her mind wandered unbidden to thoughts of Jacob.

She shook her head, attempting to banish the intrusive thoughts. *Focus, Leah,* she chided herself silently. *These people are counting on you.* Yet even as she redoubled her efforts, Jacob's gentle smile and kind eyes lingered in her mind's eye, a bittersweet reminder of the feelings she had tried so hard to suppress.

Across town, Rachel strode purposefully through the bustling streets, her high heels clicking rhythmically against the pavement. She clutched a binder overflowing with fabric swatches, vendor contracts, and seating charts—the culmination of weeks of meticulous planning. As she navigated the crowded sidewalks, Rachel's thoughts were consumed by visions of her impending nuptials, each detail meticulously crafted to showcase the perfect union of two successful, influential families.

Lost in thought, Rachel hardly noticed the strained expression on Jacob's face as he walked beside her, his silence drowned out by the cacophony of the city. She chattered incessantly about floral arrangements and catering options, oblivious to the growing distance between them. Jacob's half-hearted responses went unnoticed as Rachel pressed onward, determined to orchestrate a wedding that would be the talk of their social circle for years to come.

As the sun dipped below the horizon, Leah finally set aside her work, rubbing her eyes wearily. She gazed out the small window of her office, watching as the city lights flickered to life in the gathering dusk. In the stillness of the evening, Leah allowed herself a moment to acknowledge the ache in her heart—the longing for a love she knew could never be. With a sigh, she gathered her belongings and stepped out into the night, steeling herself to face another day of burying her feelings beneath the weight of her responsibilities.

Jacob found himself at a quiet park bench, seeking solace from the whirlwind of wedding preparations. The gentle rustling of leaves in the warm breeze seemed to whisper secrets of the heart, urging him to confront the truth he had been denying. As he sat, lost in thought, a familiar figure approached—Leah, her presence a soothing balm to his troubled soul.

"Jacob," Leah greeted softly, her voice a melodic contrast to the chaos that had consumed his life in recent weeks. "Is everything alright?"

He met her gaze, finding in her eyes a depth of

understanding that reached into the very core of his being. "I don't know anymore, Leah. I thought I had it all figured out, but now..." His words trailed off, the unspoken hanging heavily in the air between them.

Leah sat beside him, her presence a silent invitation to unburden his heart. "Sometimes, the path we think we're meant to follow isn't the one that leads to true happiness," she said, her words a gentle echo of the doubts that had taken root in Jacob's mind.

As they talked, Jacob found himself drawn to the quiet strength that emanated from Leah—a strength born of compassion, resilience, and an unwavering commitment to those she loved. In the warmth of her presence, he began to see the beauty that had always been there, hidden beneath the shadow of her sister's vibrant charm.

"Leah," Jacob said, his voice barely above a whisper, "I think I've been so focused on the life I thought I wanted that I haven't been true to myself. And now, sitting here with you, I realize that what I've been searching for has been right in front of me all along."

Leah's heart raced at his words, a bittersweet mix of hope and trepidation washing over her. She had long since resigned herself to a life in Rachel's shadow, convinced that her own desires would forever remain unspoken. Yet here, in this moment of vulnerability, she saw a glimmer of possibility—a chance for a love that could weather any storm.

As the sun began to set, casting a golden glow over the park, Jacob and Leah sat in silence, each lost in their own thoughts. The future stretched out before them, uncertain and uncharted, but in the quiet understanding that passed between them, they found the courage to face whatever lay ahead, together.

CHAPTER 6

Jacob took a sip of champagne, his eyes scanning the glittering ballroom filled with Seattle's elite gathered for the annual charity gala. Across the room, he spotted Leah, her simple dress again a stark contrast to the opulent attire of the other guests. She looked lost in thought, her gentle features etched with a touch of melancholy. Setting his glass on a passing waiter's tray, Jacob wove through the crowd toward her.

"Penny for your thoughts," he said softly, coming to stand beside her.

Leah startled slightly, then offered him a wan smile. "Oh, Jacob. I didn't see you there." She fidgeted with the delicate silver cross at her throat, a nervous tell he'd come to recognize.

"Is everything alright? You seem...pensive tonight."

She hesitated, her hazel eyes searching his. In their depths, he saw a flicker of some unspoken emotion. Fear, perhaps. Or longing. "There's something I need to tell you," she began, her voice barely above a whisper. "Something I've been holding inside for a long time."

Jacob's brow furrowed with concern, but he remained silent, allowing her the space to gather her thoughts. Around them, the tinkling laughter and clinking glasses faded into the background, the moment suspended in time.

Leah drew a shaky breath. "The truth is, Jacob...I have feelings for you. Feelings that go beyond friendship." A blush bloomed on her cheeks, and she quickly averted her gaze. "I know it's wrong. You're with Rachel, and I would never want to come between you. But I can't keep pretending anymore."

Jacob felt a wave of conflicting emotions wash over him. Surprise, certainly. A twinge of guilt. And beneath it all, a troubling spark of something else entirely. Something he wasn't ready to acknowledge.

Before he could formulate a response, a sharp

gasp pierced the air behind them. He turned to see Rachel standing there, her elegant features contorted with shock and betrayal. In her hand, a half-empty champagne flute trembled precariously.

"How could you?" she hissed, her voice low and venomous. She stalked forward, closing the distance between them in a few purposeful strides. "My own sister, trying to steal my boyfriend. I should have known you'd stoop so low, Leah."

Leah recoiled as if slapped, her eyes brimming with unshed tears. "Rachel, please. It's not what you think. I would never-"

"Save it," Rachel snapped, holding up a perfectly manicured hand. "I heard everything. Your little confession. Well, let me make one thing perfectly clear." She turned to Jacob, her gaze hard and unyielding. "If you choose her, we're through. I won't be made a fool of, not by anyone. Least of all my own flesh and blood."

With that, she spun on her heel and stalked away, leaving a trail of shocked whispers in her wake. Jacob stood frozen, both shocked by the revelation that the two women he was so drawn to were sisters and torn between the urge to go after Rachel and the need to comfort Leah, who had crumpled into a nearby chair, her shoulders shaking with silent sobs.

In that moment, with the weight of two hearts in his hands, Jacob felt the full burden of the choices that lay ahead. Choices that would inevitably leave someone broken. And as he looked out over the sea of oblivious partygoers, their laughter now grating and hollow, he couldn't help but wonder if any of it was worth the price of love.

Leah sat at her desk, the blank page before her a grim reflection of the emptiness she felt inside. The decision to distance herself from both Rachel and Jacob had been the hardest she'd ever made, but also the most necessary. She couldn't continue living in her sister's shadow, constantly comparing herself and coming up short. Nor could she bear the weight of her unrequited feelings for Jacob, knowing that his heart belonged to another.

With a heavy sigh, she picked up her pen and began to write, pouring her tangled emotions onto the page. The words flowed like a river, carrying with them the pain, the longing, and the desperate need for self-discovery that had driven her to this moment.

As the days turned into weeks, Leah threw herself into her work, volunteering at the local community center and taking classes in photography, a long-forgotten passion. Slowly but surely, she began to rediscover parts of herself that had been lost in the constant struggle to measure up. She found solace in the smiles of the children she tutored, in the beauty of a perfectly captured moment, and in the quiet strength that grew within her each day.

Yet even as she flourished, Leah couldn't help but feel the absence of Rachel and Jacob like a persistent ache. She heard whispers of their strained relationship, the tension that had grown between them in the wake of her departure. Part of her longed to reach out, to mend the bridges she had burned, but a larger part knew that this journey was one she had to take alone.

One evening, as she sat on her balcony watching the sun sink below the horizon, Leah felt a sense of peace wash over her. She knew that the road ahead would be long and difficult, that there would be moments of doubt and fear. But for the first time in her life, she also knew that she was strong enough to face them, to stand on her own two feet and carve out a path that was uniquely hers.

With a soft smile, she closed her eyes and let the warm breeze caress her face, carrying with it the promise of a brighter tomorrow. And though the future was uncertain, Leah knew that she would face it with grace, with courage, and with the unshakable belief that she was worthy of love, both from others and from herself.

CHAPTER 7

Leah sat at her small wooden desk, the glow of her laptop screen illuminating her pensive face as she typed intently. Her fingers danced across the keys, pouring her heart into the grant proposal that could secure funding for a new youth mentorship program. The tiny office was a haven, a place where she could channel her passions into something meaningful.

As she paused to review her work, a subtle smile played at the corners of her lips. The words on the screen reflected her growth, her newfound sense of purpose. She had spent so long in the shadows, yearning for a love that seemed just out of reach. But now, as she immersed herself in her calling, she felt a flicker of something new—contentment.

Leah's reverie was interrupted by a soft knock at the door. "Come in," she called, her voice warm and inviting.

Jacob stepped into the office, his presence filling the small space. "Hey, Leah. Got a minute?"

She nodded, gesturing for him to take a seat. As he settled into the chair across from her, Leah studied his face. There was a weariness in his eyes, a heaviness that seemed to weigh on his broad shoulders.

"What's on your mind, Jacob?" she asked gently, her eyes searching his.

He sighed, running a hand through his hair. "I've been thinking a lot lately, about...everything. About my life, my choices." His voice trailed off, and he looked down at his hands.

Leah waited patiently, giving him space to gather his thoughts. She knew Jacob, knew the depth of his soul. She had seen it in the way he cared for others, in the passion he poured into his culinary creations.

"I'm starting to wonder if I've been chasing the wrong things," he continued, his voice barely above a whisper. "The glamour, the ambition. It all seems so hollow now."

Leah's heart ached for him. She understood

the allure of the spotlight, the desire to prove oneself. But she also knew the peace that came with embracing one's true path.

"What is it that you really want, Jacob?" she asked softly, her voice a gentle prod.

He met her gaze then, his blue eyes filled with a swirl of emotions. "I want...I want something real. Something honest." His words hung in the air, heavy with unspoken meaning.

Leah felt a flicker of hope in her chest, but she tamped it down. She had made her peace, had chosen to move forward. She couldn't let herself fall back into old patterns.

"Sometimes," she said carefully, "we have to let go of what we thought we wanted, in order to embrace what we truly need."

Jacob nodded slowly, his eyes never leaving hers. "I think I'm starting to understand that now."

As they sat there in the quiet of the office, the weight of their shared history hung between them. But there was also a new lightness, a sense of possibility. They had both grown, both begun to find their own way.

And as Leah turned back to her work, she felt a sense of peace wash over her. She had found her place in the world, had learned to love herself first.

Whatever the future held, she knew she would face it with grace and strength.

Rachel stood at the floor-to-ceiling window of her penthouse apartment, the city lights twinkling below like a sea of stars. In her hand, a glass of pinot noir, the rich burgundy liquid untouched. Her reflection stared back at her, a perfect image of success and sophistication. But behind the flawless makeup and designer dress, her eyes held a hollowness she could no longer ignore.

She thought of Jacob, of the way he'd looked at Leah with such tenderness, such understanding. In all their time together, had he ever looked at her that way? Had she ever given him reason to?

A single tear slipped down her cheek, leaving a trail of mascara in its wake. She brushed it away impatiently, angry at her own weakness. This wasn't who she was supposed to be. She was Rachel White, the woman who had it all, who never let anything or anyone stand in her way.

But standing there, alone in her pristine apartment, she felt a creeping sense of emptiness, of dissatisfaction. She had spent so long climbing the ladder, chasing after the next big win, the next accolade. But what had it all been for?

She thought of her friends, the ones she had pushed away in her relentless pursuit of success. She thought of her family, the relationships she had neglected in favor of late nights at the office and networking events. Had it all been worth it?

"No," she whispered to herself, the word harsh in the stillness of the room. "It hasn't."

She set her glass down on the window sill, the wine sloshing gently against the sides. She needed to make a change, to find a way back to the things that truly mattered. It wouldn't be easy, but she knew now that it was necessary.

With a deep breath, she turned away from the window, away from the glittering facade of her life. She had some apologies to make, some bridges to mend. And for the first time in a long time, she felt a flicker of hope, of possibility.

Maybe it wasn't too late to find something real, something honest. Maybe it wasn't too late to find herself.

CHAPTER 8

Rachel's heels clicked on the polished hardwood floor as she made her way towards Leah, who sat quietly on her living room couch, her hands folded in her lap. The late afternoon sun streamed through the windows, casting a warm glow on Leah's gentle features. Rachel took a deep breath, her usual air of confidence wavering as she approached her sister.

"Leah," Rachel began, her voice softer than usual, "I owe you an apology." She sat down beside Leah, the leather cushions sighing beneath her weight. "My behavior earlier was unacceptable. I let my own insecurities get the best of me, and I took it out on you. That wasn't fair."

Leah turned to face her sister, her brow furrowed in thought. She studied Rachel's face, noting the vulnerability that shone in her emerald eyes—a rare glimpse behind the polished façade. "I appreciate your apology, Rachel," Leah replied, her tone warm and sincere. "I know our relationship hasn't always been easy, but I want you to know that I've never stopped caring about you."

Rachel felt a lump form in her throat, the weight of their shared history pressing down upon her. She had spent so long striving for perfection, for the acclaim and recognition that came with being the family's golden child. But in that pursuit, she had left Leah in the shadows, overlooked and undervalued. "I've been so focused on my own goals that I've neglected what truly matters," Rachel confessed, her voice thick with emotion. "I'm sorry, Leah. I want to make things right between us."

Leah reached out, placing a comforting hand on Rachel's arm. "I forgive you, Rachel. We're sisters, and that bond is stronger than any disagreement or misunderstanding." She smiled, the warmth of her expression like a balm to Rachel's troubled heart. "Let's start fresh, shall we?"

Rachel nodded, a tentative smile tugging at the corners of her lips. "I'd like that very much."

As the sisters embraced, the sun dipped lower

on the horizon, its golden rays painting the room in a soft, forgiving light. It was a moment of reconciliation, a first step towards healing the rift that had grown between them. Though the path ahead was uncertain, Rachel felt a glimmer of hope and the promise of a new beginning.

Jacob stood before Rachel, his hands clasped together, his brow furrowed in contemplation. The bustling café around them faded into the background as he focused on the words he needed to say. "Rachel," he began, his voice steady despite the turmoil within, "there's something I need to tell you."

Rachel looked up at him, her green eyes searching his face for clues. She had sensed a change in Jacob over the past few weeks, a growing distance that she couldn't quite explain. "What is it, Jacob?" she asked, her tone measured and calm.

Jacob took a deep breath, steeling himself for the difficult conversation ahead. "I've been doing a lot of thinking about our relationship, about our future together." He paused, choosing his words carefully. "I admire you, Rachel. Your ambition, your drive—it's truly remarkable. But I've come to realize that we want different things out of life."

Rachel felt a tightness in her chest, a sinking sensation that she couldn't ignore. She had known, deep down, that their paths were diverging, but hearing the words aloud made it all too real. "What are you saying, Jacob?" she asked, her voice barely above a whisper.

"I'm saying that I can't go through with our engagement," Jacob replied, his tone gentle but firm. "It wouldn't be fair to either of us to continue down this path when our hearts aren't fully aligned."

Rachel closed her eyes for a moment, letting the weight of his words sink in. She had always prided herself on being in control, on having a plan for every aspect of her life. But now, faced with the unexpected, she found herself surprisingly at peace. "I understand, Jacob," she said, opening her eyes to meet his gaze. "You're right. We both deserve to be with someone who loves us unconditionally, who shares our dreams and aspirations."

Jacob nodded, a flicker of relief passing over his features. "I'm glad you feel that way, Rachel. I truly want the best for you, even if that means we go our separate ways."

As they stood to leave, Rachel felt a newfound sense of clarity, a realization that had been lurking beneath the surface all along. She deserved more than a love that was half-hearted, more than a future that was shaped by compromise. And as she walked out of the café, her head held high, she knew that this ending was merely the beginning of a new chapter —one that she would write on her own terms.

Leah stood by the window, her gaze fixed on the bustling city street below. The gentle hum of conversation filled the quaint coffee shop, a soothing backdrop to the tumultuous thoughts swirling within her mind. She sensed Jacob's presence before she saw him, his footsteps a familiar rhythm against the hardwood floor.

"Leah," he said softly, his voice a caress that sent a shiver down her spine. She turned to face him, her heart skipping a beat as their eyes met. In the warm glow of the afternoon sun, Jacob looked every bit the successful entrepreneur, his tailored suit a stark contrast to the vulnerability that shone in his piercing blue eyes.

"Jacob," she breathed, her own voice barely above a whisper. "I wasn't sure you'd come."

He took a step closer, his hand reaching out to brush a stray lock of hair from her face. "I couldn't stay away," he admitted, his touch lingering on her cheek. "Not after everything that's happened."

Leah leaned into his touch, her eyes fluttering closed for a brief moment. How easy it would be, she thought, to lose herself in the warmth of his embrace, to forget the obstacles that stood between them. But she knew that they couldn't ignore the truth any longer.

"We can't do this, Jacob," she said, her voice trembling with emotion. "We both know that our lives are headed in different directions."

Jacob sighed, his shoulders sagging under the weight of her words. "I know," he said, his gaze dropping to the floor. "But I can't help the way I feel about you, Leah. You've always been there for me, even when I didn't deserve it."

Leah's heart ached at the pain in his voice, the raw honesty that stripped away the layers of his carefully constructed facade. She reached out to take his hand, her fingers intertwining with his.

"You do deserve it, Jacob," she said firmly, her eyes shining with unshed tears. "You deserve to be happy, to find someone who can give you the life you've always wanted."

Jacob looked up at her then, his eyes searching her face for the truth behind her words. "And what about you, Leah?" he asked, his voice barely above a whisper. "What do you want?"

The question hung heavy in the air between them, a reminder of the unspoken feelings that had always lingered just beneath the surface. Leah took a deep breath, her heart racing as she summoned the courage to speak the words that had been trapped inside her for so long.

"I want you to be happy, Jacob," she said, her voice steady despite the tears that threatened to fall. "Even if that means letting you go."

Jacob nodded, his eyes glistening with emotion. "I want that for you too, Leah," he said, his thumb brushing gently over the back of her hand. "More than anything."

They stood there for a moment, their hands clasped together, their hearts beating in unison. And then, with a final squeeze of her fingers, Jacob let go, his footsteps echoing as he walked away.

Leah watched him go, her heart aching with

the bittersweet realization that sometimes, love meant putting someone else's happiness before your own. She turned back to the window, her gaze once again fixed on the city below. And as the sun began to set, casting a golden glow over the bustling streets, she knew that this was not the end of their story, but merely the beginning of a new chapter—one that they would write together, even if it was from afar.

CHAPTER 9

Rachel gazed out the floor-to-ceiling windows of her corner office, the bustling city streets below a blur of motion and purpose. The sky was a muted gray, clouds heavy with the promise of rain. She absently fingered the silver cross pendant at her throat, a gift from her grandmother when she first started at the firm. It had been her talisman, a reminder of her roots and her faith, even as she climbed the corporate ladder with single-minded determination.

But now, standing at the pinnacle of success, Rachel felt a hollowness inside her that no amount of accolades or bonuses could fill. The long hours, the cutthroat competition, the endless striving—it had consumed her life, leaving little room for anything else. Her relationships had suffered, her health had declined, and her soul felt parched, thirsting for something more substantial than fleeting worldly triumphs.

With a sigh, Rachel turned from the window and settled into her leather executive chair. She picked up the framed photo on her desk - a candid shot of her and her sisters, laughing together at a family picnic. Their faces were alight with joy and love, untouched by the cares of adulthood. Rachel traced their smiles with a wistful finger, a pang of longing piercing her heart. When had she last felt that carefree, that connected to the people who mattered most?

A knock at the door startled her from her reverie. "Come in," she called, straightening in her seat.

Her assistant, Maggie, poked her head in. "Sorry to disturb you, Ms. White, but I wanted to remind you about the strategic planning meeting at 2 o'clock."

Rachel glanced at her watch, the diamond-encrusted face winking up at her. "Thank you, Maggie. I'll be there."

Maggie hesitated, her eyes filled with concern. "Is everything alright, Ms. White? You seem...preoccupied lately."

Rachel forced a smile, the mask of professionalism slipping back into place. "I'm fine, Maggie. Just a lot on my mind with the new product launch coming up."

Maggie nodded, but the worry didn't leave her face. "Of course. Well, if you need anything, just let me know."

As the door clicked shut behind her, Rachel leaned back in her chair, her gaze drifting once more to the gray skies beyond the window. The restlessness inside her was growing, a yearning for something more than the empty pursuit of worldly success. She thought of the countless Sundays spent in church as a child, the peace and purpose she had found in serving others and living out her faith. Somewhere along the way, she had lost sight of what truly mattered, seduced by the siren song of ambition and acclaim.

Rachel closed her eyes, a silent prayer forming on her lips. "Lord, guide me. Show me how to use the gifts You've given me to make a real difference in this world. Help me find the balance between work and faith, between success and significance."

As if in answer, a ray of sunlight pierced the clouds, bathing her office in a warm, golden glow. Rachel felt a flicker of hope ignite within her, a whisper of divine guidance. She knew it wouldn't be easy, reorienting her life and her priorities, but she also knew it was necessary—for her own soul, and for the greater good.

With renewed determination, Rachel pulled out a fresh notebook and began to write, the words flowing from some deep wellspring inside her. A new project, one that would combine her marketing savvy with her Christian values, to create something truly meaningful and impactful. She didn't have all the details yet, but she trusted that God would reveal the path, step by step.

As she wrote, Rachel felt a lightness suffusing her being, a sense of rightness and purpose that had eluded her for so long. This was what she was meant to do, what she was called to be. Not just a successful executive, but a woman of faith, using her talents to glorify God and serve His people.

The rain began to fall outside, a gentle patter against the windows, but Rachel barely noticed. She was too caught up in the vision unfolding before her, a future filled with hope and meaning, guided by the unwavering love of her Heavenly Father. Whatever challenges lay ahead, she knew she would face them with grace and strength, secure in the knowledge that she was exactly where she was meant to be.

Leah stood at the window of her modest apartment, watching the golden hues of the sunset paint the city skyline. The fading light seemed to mirror the gradual transformation within her, a slow but steady shift from self-doubt to self-acceptance. Her hands cradled a steaming mug of chamomile tea, the warmth seeping into her palms, a gentle reminder of the comfort she'd learned to find in solitude.

The past few months had been a journey of introspection and growth, a path she'd embarked upon with trepidation but now walked with increasing confidence. She'd always been the quiet one, the overshadowed sister, but in the stillness of her own company, Leah had begun to discover a strength she'd never known she possessed.

Her work at the social services agency had become more than just a job. It was a calling, a way to channel her empathy and compassion into tangible change. Each small victory, each smile on the face of a child she'd helped, felt like a step towards a greater purpose.

Leah's gaze drifted to the Bible on her night-stand, its well-worn pages a testament to the hours she'd spent seeking guidance and solace in its words. She'd always had faith, but it was only now that she truly understood its depth, the way it could anchor her in the midst of life's uncertainties.

As she sipped her tea, Leah's thoughts turned to her sister, Rachel. They'd always been different, but lately, there seemed to be a new understanding between them, a recognition of the unique paths they'd chosen. Leah no longer felt the need to measure herself against Rachel's achievements. Her own accomplishments, quiet though they might be, were no less significant.

The chime of her phone interrupted her musings. Glancing at the screen, Leah saw a message from one of her colleagues, praising her handling of a particularly challenging case. A smile tugged at her lips, a testament to the validation she'd learned to find from within.

Setting down her mug, Leah moved to her small desk, where a stack of case files awaited her attention. There was still so much work to be done, so many lives to touch, but she no longer felt daunted by the task. She'd found her calling, her place in the world, and with each passing day, she grew more certain of her ability to make a difference.

As she settled into her chair, Leah whispered a silent prayer, thanking God for the strength He'd given her, for the peace she'd found in His love. Whatever the future held, she knew she would face it with grace and resilience, secure in the knowledge that her worth came not from the opinions of others, but from the unshakable foundation of her faith.

Jacob stood at the window of his empty apartment, the city skyline stretching out before him like a tapestry of memories. The sun's last rays painted the sky in shades of orange and pink, a bittersweet farewell to the life he'd built here. He sighed, his breath fogging the glass, as he contemplated the journey ahead.

The decision to leave hadn't been easy, but Jacob knew it was time for a change. His restaurants had become a well-oiled machine, no longer requiring his constant presence, and the restlessness in his soul had grown too loud to ignore. He needed a new challenge, a fresh canvas upon which to paint the next chapter of his life.

With a final glance around the room, Jacob picked up his suitcase and headed for the door. As he stepped into the hallway, his phone buzzed with incoming messages from Rachel and Leah, both wishing him well on his new venture. A smile tugged at the corners of his mouth, warmed by their support and understanding.

I'll keep in touch, and I'll be back to visit, I promise.

Hitting send, Jacob pocketed his phone and made his way to the elevator. The doors slid open, and he stepped inside, his reflection staring back at him from the polished metal. In that moment, he saw not only the man he was, but the man he hoped to become—a little wiser, a little more humble, and a lot more grateful for the blessings in his life.

As the elevator descended, Jacob closed his eyes and whispered a prayer, entrusting his future to God's hands. He didn't know what lay ahead, but he had faith that everything would work out as it was meant to. And though his relationships with Rachel and Leah remained undefined, he knew that the love and respect they shared would endure, no matter where their paths might lead.

The doors opened, and Jacob stepped out into the lobby, his footsteps echoing on the marble floor. With a deep breath, he pushed through the revolving door and emerged onto the bustling street, ready to embrace the unknown and discover what the world had in store for him.

The sun dappled through the rustling leaves overhead, casting a warm glow across the quaint garden patio where Rachel and Leah sat, a pot of fragrant lavender tea steeping between them. The delicate clink of china teacups punctuated their gentle laughter as they reminisced, the trials and heartaches of months past now softened by time's healing touch.

Rachel leaned back, her elegant fingers absently tracing the gilded rim of her teacup. "I never imagined we'd find ourselves here, Leah. After everything..." Her words trailed off, a wistful smile playing at the corners of her lips.

Leah reached out, her hand resting gently atop her sister's. "We've grown so much, haven't we? Both of us." Her warm brown eyes sparkled with a newfound wisdom, the scars of self-doubt and insecurity now faded and nearly forgotten.

As the afternoon lengthened, the sisters fell into a comfortable silence, each lost in their own thoughts. Rachel's mind wandered to the challenges she'd faced, the walls she'd built around her heart crumbling brick by brick as she learned to embrace vulnerability, to find strength in the support of those who loved her unconditionally. Leah, too, reflected on her journey, the quiet resilience that had carried her through the darkest of days now a glowing ember within her soul, a constant reminder of her own worth and value.

The tranquil moment was broken by the chime of Leah's phone, a message illuminating the screen. Her brow furrowed slightly as she read the words, a flicker of surprise dancing across her delicate features.

"It's Jacob," she murmured, a hint of wonder in her voice. "He's back in town and wants to meet up."

Rachel arched an eyebrow, a knowing smile tugging at her lips. "And? What will you do?"

Leah paused, considering the question. In the months since their last encounter, she'd found a new sense of self, a quiet confidence that radiated from within. No longer content to be a mere footnote in another's story, she knew that any path forward would be on her terms, and her terms alone.

With a soft smile, Leah met her sister's gaze, a glimmer of possibility shining in her eyes. "I think," she began, her voice steady and sure, "that I'll see where this road leads. But this time, I'll be the one holding the map."

Rachel nodded, pride and understanding etched across her face. They had both come so far, each forging their own path through the wilderness of the heart. And now, as the sun began its slow descent toward the horizon, the future stretched out before them, a canvas of infinite possibility, waiting to be painted in the vibrant hues of their own choosing.

As the sun dipped behind the city skyline, Rachel and Leah walked side by side through the bustling streets, their steps in perfect harmony. The trials of the past, the heartaches and uncertainties, had slowly faded into memory, replaced by a deep, unshakable bond that transcended the boundaries of sisterhood.

Leah breathed in the crisp evening air, her heart swelling with a newfound sense of peace.

The message from Jacob, once a source of trepidation, now felt like a distant echo, a reminder of the person she used to be. She glanced at Rachel, marveling at the strength and resilience that emanated from her sister's every move.

"You know," Leah said softly, her words carried on the gentle breeze, "I used to think that happiness was something to be found in the arms of another. That without love, I would never be complete."

Rachel nodded, her eyes glistening with understanding. "And now?" she asked, her voice a tender caress.

Leah smiled, a radiant expression that spoke of hard-won wisdom. "Now, I know that true happiness comes from within. It's in the quiet moments, the small victories, and the love we have for ourselves."

They continued their walk, the city's pulse thrumming beneath their feet. The skyscrapers, once towering monuments to Rachel's ambition, now seemed to bow in reverence to the unbreakable connection between the two sisters.

"I'm proud of us," Rachel said, her voice thick with emotion. "We've faced our demons, confronted our fears, and emerged stronger than ever."

Leah reached out, her hand finding Rachel's, their fingers intertwining in a silent affirmation of their bond. "Together," she whispered, her words a sacred vow.

As the last rays of sunlight painted the world in a warm, golden glow, Rachel and Leah walked on, their laughter echoing through the streets. They had found their true north, not in the promise of romance, but in the unshakable foundation of self-love and sisterhood. And with each step, they knew that no matter what the future held, they would face it together, forever united in the unbreakable bonds of the heart.

EXCERPT FROM HANNAH

Hannah's gaze drifted from the flickering computer screen to the framed photo on her desk—a candid shot of her and James, their smiles radiant with hope and possibility. The image seemed to belong to another lifetime, a world untouched by the weight of their shared longing. She clicked through the endless stream of baby announcements and gender reveals, each one a bittersweet reminder of the joy that remained just beyond her grasp.

A knock at the door pulled her back to the present. "Hannah, the meeting is starting in five minutes," her assistant reminded her gently.

"Thank you, I'll be right there," Hannah replied, her voice steady despite the tempest brewing within. She straightened her blazer, a suit of armor against the well-meaning inquiries and sympathetic glances that awaited her in the conference room.

As she navigated the labyrinth of cubicles, Hannah's thoughts drifted to the appointment she and James had scheduled for that afternoon. Another round of tests, another glimmer of hope to cling to in the face of mounting disappointment. She silently recited a prayer, a plea for strength and guidance, as she took her seat at the long table.

The meeting passed in a blur of sales projections and market analyses, the numbers dancing before her eyes like distant constellations. Hannah forced herself to focus, to contribute, to prove that she was more than the sum of her unfulfilled desires. She felt James's absence keenly, longing for the reassuring warmth of his hand in hers.

***

Hours later, they sat side by side in the waiting room, the sterile white walls closing in on them like an arctic landscape. James's leg bounced nervously, a staccato rhythm that echoed the pounding of Hannah's heart. She reached for his hand, intertwining their fingers, a silent affirmation of their unbreakable bond.

The doctor entered, his expression a carefully crafted mask of professional detachment. "I'm sorry," he began, the words hanging heavy in the air. "The latest round of treatment was unsuccessful."

Hannah felt the room tilt, the ground shifting beneath her feet. James's grip tightened, anchoring her to the present. "What are our options?" he asked, his voice strained but resolute.

As the doctor outlined the next steps, the slim chances, and the mounting costs, Hannah felt a wave of exhaustion wash over her. The weight of their shared struggle, the countless prayers whispered in the dark, the dreams deferred and the plans put on hold—it all seemed to coalesce in that moment, a burden too heavy to bear alone.

Yet, as they walked out of the clinic, hand in hand, Hannah felt a flicker of something else—a quiet resilience, a stubborn hope that refused to be extinguished. She leaned into James, drawing strength from his steady presence, and together they stepped out into the uncertain future, their faith a guiding light in the gathering darkness.

***

The next morning, Hannah stepped into the office, her heart still heavy from the previous day's news. She made her way to her desk, the familiar bustle of the workplace washing over her. She immersed herself in her work, finding solace in the routine, the tasks at hand offering a temporary reprieve from the turmoil within.

Miriam's voice cut through the hum of activity, drawing everyone's attention. "Guys, I have an announcement to make!" Her face was radiant, her eyes sparkling with unbridled joy. "I'm pregnant!"

The room erupted in a chorus of congratulations, colleagues swarming around Miriam, offering hugs and well wishes. Hannah felt a sharp pang in her chest, a bittersweet mixture of happiness for her friend and a profound sense of loss. She plastered a smile on her face, joining the throng of well-wishers.

"Congratulations, Miriam," Hannah said, her voice wavering slightly as she embraced her colleague. "I'm so happy for you."

Miriam beamed, her hand instinctively resting on her still-flat stomach. "Thank you, Hannah. It's been such a journey, but we're thrilled."

Hannah nodded, swallowing past the lump in her throat. She knew all too well the weight of that journey, the endless cycles of hope and disappointment. As the conversation shifted to due dates and baby showers, Hannah quietly excused herself, slipping away to the sanctuary of the restroom.

In the harsh fluorescent light, Hannah gripped the edges of the sink, her knuckles turning white. She stared at her reflection, the woman looking back at her a stranger—hollow-eyed and fragile. The tears came then, hot and fast, spilling down her cheeks in silent rivulets.

"Why, God?" she whispered, her voice barely audible over the hum of the ventilation. "Why does it have to be this hard?"

She closed her eyes, drawing in a shuddering breath. In the stillness, a small voice seemed to whisper back, a gentle reminder of the faith that had carried her this far. *Trust in My plan, even when you cannot see the path ahead.*

Hannah let the words wash over her, a balm to her aching soul. She wiped away her tears, straightening her shoulders. She knew the road ahead would be difficult, the pain of this moment just one of many she would have to endure. But she also knew that she was not alone, that her faith and the love of those around her would be her strength.

With a final glance in the mirror, Hannah stepped out of the restroom, ready to face the day ahead. The weight of her struggle was still there, but so too was the flicker of hope, the unshakeable belief that somehow, someday, her prayers would be answered.

Get Hannah: A Modern Tale of Love and Faith now!

ABOUT THE AUTHOR

Award-winning author Kayla Lowe writes women's fiction that explores complex themes with sensitivity and depth. Kayla's books delve into the intricacies of relationships, self-discovery, and resilience. From cozy love stories interspersed with a bit of faith to heartwarming tales of friendship and suspenseful novels of empowerment and heartbreak, her books illustrate the struggles specific to women.

When she's not churning out her next novel, you can find her with her feet in the sand and a book in her hand or curled up on the couch with her dogs.

Visit her website at www.authorkaylalowe.com.

ALSO BY KAYLA LOWE

<u>Series</u>

<u>Charms of the Chaste Court</u>

A Courtship in Covent Garden

Whispers in Westminster

Romance in Regent's Park

Serenade on Strand Street

Treasure in Tower Bridge

<u>Sweet Honey by the Sea</u>

<u>The Beekeeper's Secret (Book 1)</u>

<u>A Royal Honeycomb (Book 2)</u>

<u>Bees in Blossom (Book 3)</u>

<u>Honeyed Kisses (Book 4)</u>

<u>Blooming Forever (Book 5)</u>

<u>Strawberry Beach Series</u>

<u>Beachside Lessons (Book 1)</u>

<u>Beachside Lessons (Book 2)</u>

<u>Beachside Lessons (Book 3)</u>

Panama City Beach Series

Sun-Kissed Secrets (Book 1)

Sun-Kissed Secrets (Book 2)

Sun-Kissed Secrets (Book 3)

The Tainted Love Saga

Of Love and Deception (Book 1)

Of Love and Family (Book 2)

Of Love and Violence (Book 3)

Of Love and Abuse (Book 4)

Of Love and Crime (Book 5)

Of Love and Addiction (Book 6)

Of Love and Redemption (Book 7)

<u>Standalones</u>

Maiden's Blush

<u>Poetry</u>

Phantom Poetry

Lost and Found